CREATURE LOVING VOLUME 6: A MONSTER EROTICA COLLECTION

Lilith Leana

Table of Contents

Acknowledgement

A big thank you to my husband for always believing in me and never making me feel like I couldn't do it.

Cover art

Cover art photo from Depositphoto

Cover design

Lilith Leana with Canva

Brief Summary

Nesting with the Shifter

Vanya is an Omega Wolf shifter who suddenly feels the need to nest. In a remote mountain cabin, she carefully arranges her nest, preparing for her fated Mate's arrival.

Kai is a Mountain Lion shifter passing through when he smells his Mate. He wants to help her build her nest and fill it with pups and cubs.

Chased by the Gargoyle

With a mix of anticipation and uncertainty, Sadie arrives at her first monthly Human-Monster mixer. Little does she know, her evening is about to take an unexpected turn when a captivating Gargoyle sets his sights on her, his intentions extending far beyond just a chase.

As Sadie heads to the Human-Monster Mixer, William sees it as the ideal moment to finally reveal his interest in her, after secretly watching her for a while. The moment he tastes her, he realizes he can't let her slip away from his grasp.

Saved by the Kraken

Isla nearly loses her life when her oxygen tank malfunctions while diving. Luckily a Kraken saw her in time and took her to his cave. She is grateful to him for saving her life, and asks him what he wants in return. He only wants one taste, but one soon turns to more.

Jax has always found humans curious, but kept his distance, until a pretty little human almost drowns outside of his cave, forcing him to save her. Her scent fascinates him, and he wants to taste her, but the moment his lips touch her, he knows he needs more than just one taste.

Interviewing the Yeti

Charlotte's one focus is on getting the interview of her career, but when she meets the gorgeous Yeti clan leader she is interviewing, she suddenly can't seem to remember anything except how his gorgeous blue eyes make her feel.

Trent the Yeti immediately feels drawn to the human interviewer who is visiting his clan. He just hopes he can convince her to stay with him when the interview is over and she has everything she came to his clan for.

Meeting with my Mate

Scarlett is frantically rushing to the most important meeting of her life, after the best wet dream she's ever had. When the man she is meeting turns out to be the Mate she was dreaming about, her morning takes a very different turn.

Shane has been looking for his Mate for so long, that he never expected to see her stand before him in his meeting room. One look at her, and he knows he will never let her go. He needs to claim her immediately.

Moving in with the Naga

Ezra and Avery are moving in together and breaking in their new bed.

READER ADVISORY: THIS story contains explicit sex scenes.

Creature Loving Volume 6 is a collection of five previously published standalone short erotic stories and one exciting new bonus story.

It is filled with human FMC's loving Monsters, Beasts and Creatures. Explicit sex scenes, standalone, no cheating or cliffhangers.

Nesting with the Shifter

I was nesting, and it was embarrassing. I was a 36-year-old unmated Omega and I shouldn't nest without a Mate, but apparently, my wolf hadn't gotten the memo. Luckily, my Alpha was understanding and gave me a month off from my duties so I could go to a cabin deep in the woods to make my nest.

So I packed up all the pillows, blankets, towels, and soft fabric that I had into my car and drove to the cabin. My wolf was eager to make the nest and mark the territory around, but I had to get all of my stuff inside before I could let her roam free. After I finished unpacking everything, I undressed and transformed into my wolf form.

I yapped happily at all the softness surrounding me. I scented everything as I moved the blankets around to make a comfortable nest for me to sleep in. The cabin was the perfect size for a couple, with one big room that included the kitchen and sleeping area with a massive fireplace. The bathroom was outside, but there was also a small stream nearby I could bathe in.

I focused on making my nest with everything I had brought. Every piece of fabric and pillow had to be placed just right to make the perfect nest, but it didn't feel right. I had to make do with what I had, missing the softness of furs that my Mate would provide. Surrounded by my comforting fabrics and pillowy cushions, I curled up, but I still felt empty inside. I needed someone to share my nest with. Someone who would mate me, breed me, and fill me with pups.

Everyone I grew up with had already mated and had a growing family, but I was all alone. My heart and womb were achingly empty. My 15th Heat was coming soon, and I wasn't sure how many more I had left in me. Being comfortable in my nest, trying to forget all my worries, made my wolf restless. I still needed to mark the surrounding territory so that everyone passing by would know not to disturb me.

I ran outside, loving the feel of the wind rushing through my fur. Brushing against every tree I encountered, I left my scent behind. When I had marked everything in a 10-mile radius, I went to the little stream to freshen up before going back to the cabin.

My run made me feel calmer and more grounded and I was happy to go back to my nest, curl up and fall asleep.

As I woke up, an unfamiliar scent filled the air around me while a gentle purring sound came from behind. When I turned around, my heart skipped a beat as I came face to face with a stunning mountain lion, its sleek fur and powerful presence taking my breath away.

Instead of the instinctive growl, I should have outed, a low whine came from my throat. I instantly recognized the mountain lion beside me as my long-awaited Mate.

His tail went up, and the purr grew louder. I've never heard a purr that made everything inside of me tingle as his did. I circled to smell him, loving the unfamiliar yet comforting smell of my Mate.

In the blink of an eye, he transformed into a handsome and very naked man. His build was muscular, but it leaned towards a more slender physique instead of the bulkiness I was familiar with from the wolves in my pack. His hair had a copper-blond shine to it and his eyes were a gorgeous green that seemed to look right through me.

"Is this for me?" he purred, motioning around to my nest.

I transformed as well, suddenly very naked under his appreciative gaze. I nodded, averting my gaze, thinking that my nest wasn't good enough for him. One finger captured my chin and pushed my eyes back up to him.

"It is perfect. I even have something that would fit here nicely," he said. "I didn't understand why I kept the fur as I tend to travel light, but now I know it was meant for you."

At the mention of a fur, my back straightened, and I had to hold in the urge to moan. My Mate would provide for me and my nest.

"Thank you, Alpha," I said.

He shook his head and made a face as if the word tasted foul. "I'm not an Alpha. I will provide for you and care for you, but we will be equal in every way. You can call me Kai. What is your name, beautiful?"

"I'm Vanya. I'm an Omega from the Wolf pack down North."

"Vanya," he almost purred my name. "Do you accept me as your Mate?"

I nodded, leaning in closer, waiting for him to kiss me.

"I really want to hear you say it, my Mate," he said, his voice lower as if he needed to contain himself not to shift.

"Yes, Kai. I accept you as my Mate."

He captured my mouth with his lips and I melted against his body. This kiss was everything I ever wanted and so much more. I had finally found my Mate, the person I would spend the rest of my life with and he accepted me and my nest even though it wasn't finished yet.

It was as if he knew my thoughts before the mating bond was even in place. He broke the kiss and gently caressed my cheek.

"Do you want me to get my furs to complete the nest?" Kai asked.

My back straightened and if I had been in wolf form, my tail would be wagging like crazy. "Only if it isn't too much effort."

"Only if I get a little taste of you before I go," my Mate groaned.

Before I could ask what he wanted to taste, he pushed me down on the furs and opened my legs wide. I moaned when his massive tongue touched my weeping pussy.

"Delicious," Kai purred against my pussy, the vibrations sparking pleasure deep inside of me.

I never imagined being with any other shifter than a wolf, but having a large cat in front of me already proved to be amazing. His tongue felt different, but oh, so good on my pussy. He licked me, tasting my wetness and purring in delight.

"Kai," I moaned as my hands went to his hair.

The soft strands tickled my fingers while his tongue did amazing things to my pussy.

"One taste will never be enough. For the rest of our lives, I'll need to taste you every day," he groaned before he dove back in between my legs.

"Yes, Kai, my Mate," I moaned as pleasure sparked with each swipe of his tongue.

His words warmed me from the inside out as my wolf howled with pleasure. After waiting for so many years, I finally found the perfect Mate. I could already see our lives together, creating one big, happy family filled with pups and cubs. Before I could wonder whose genes would be the strongest, his tongue curled around my clit, making me almost shoot out of my nest.

Kai did things with his tongue I only ever dreamed about, and when he added a finger to my tight channel, it was too much for me. I came with a scream while he happily lapped up my juices, coaxing even more pleasure out of me. My body trembled as I gripped his hair firmly in my hands and my pussy squeezed around his finger. When the tremors of my body eased, he climbed over me, looking at me with so much love in his eyes I almost choked up.

He kissed me again, my taste mingling with his in a delicious new flavor. I moaned into his mouth, wanting him, needing him here in my nest and inside of my body.

"I'll be back before you know it," Kai said and kissed me again, as if not believing that I was real. "Don't disappear on me, my Mate," he murmured against my lips.

I nipped at his lips and growled playfully. "Never."

The purr that came from his chest almost dissolved me into a puddle. I could feel it travel through my body and nestle low above my pussy, making my core contract and my pussy weep with wetness. His nostrils flared, and I knew he could smell my desire for him. I was already insatiable when it came to him. I needed him again, and again until I couldn't walk straight anymore and he had filled my womb with his seed.

With a groan and a last lingering kiss, he stood up and transformed again into the magnificent mountain lion. Without the shock of seeing an unfamiliar predator in my territory, I could admire him fully. His thick tail stood upright as he gave me a soft head bump with his cat-like face. In nature, large cats and wolves rarely mixed, but I knew that the Moon Goddess handpicked our pairing, so all would be well.

After another head bump, I petted him, earning a low purr. "Please come back soon," I said.

His large yellow eyes focused on my face, and he nodded slowly. With a sweep of his tail across my cheek, he was gone, and I fussed over my nest again. I would need to rearrange everything to make space for his fur, but I didn't know what and how many he would bring.

I started by making a fire in the gigantic fireplace in the middle of the room in front of my nest. We might not need the heat as shifters, but I loved the cozy feel of the whispering flames and the way the light played on the vaulted wooden ceiling.

Before I could truly miss him, he returned carrying a large packet in his mouth. He transformed again, and I salivated over his strong physic and massive cock. I was almost too distracted to focus on the furs but when he rolled out a massive bear skin, my inner wolf yapped happily. It was the biggest fur I had ever seen.

I immediately rolled over it, feeling the soft tendrils against my skin. With a happy sigh, I looked up at him. His eyes were burning with lust, and I knew he wouldn't be able to contain himself any longer. I quickly positioned it right in the middle of our nest, fluffing it up and surrounding it with my favorite pillows, until I finally finished my nest. Kai came up behind me, his massive body covering my small one. He sniffed at my ear and I could feel his enormous erection dig against my ass.

"Happy, my Mate?" Kai asked as he slowly ground his cock against me.

I moaned as my pussy squeezed around nothing, achingly empty and so ready to have him inside of me.

"I would be happier if you would fuck me," I moaned, biting my lip as I realized how forward I was being.

I wasn't even in heat yet and I still craved his cock more than I needed my next breath. My nest was ready and my body was, too. It was time to complete our mating bond.

"So needy," Kai purred. "Do you need my cock in your pussy?"

I gasped at his crude words, but the wetness seeping out of my pussy showed how much I loved it.

"Yes, please," I moaned.

He spread my legs wider and pushed me lower on the nest. I buried my nose in the bear's fur he had brought and I loved that it smelled like him.

"So pretty, and tight," he purred as he let his finger tease the opening of my pussy. "You think you can take all of me?" he asked.

"Yes, give it to me," I moaned, my hands gripping tightly in the fur as I arched my back to push my ass closer to him.

"I need to take care of my Mate," he said as he let one finger sink in my pussy. "But first, I need another taste."

As his mouth touched my most intimate area, a soft, guttural moan of pleasure escaped from my lips. His tongue felt amazing against my oversensitive flesh. So very different from that of a Wolf, but oh so good. I wondered what other differences there were between us. We had our whole lives to discover each other bodies and minds, learning the differences and the ways we fit together.

I loved his tongue on me, but I craved his cock deep inside of me. "Please, Kai," I moaned, my pussy clenching around nothing. "I need you inside."

"Anything for you, Vanya," he said as he positioned his cock at my entrance.

I bit back a whimper and the urge to beg him for more. He pushed in slowly, breathing heavily as if trying to contain himself, but I didn't want slow. I wanted him to ravish me, take me like a Mate should take his beloved and ruin me for any other men.

"More," I moaned as I pushed my ass closer to him, gaining another inch of his cock.

"I love to hear you beg, but I can't resist the tight clasp of your pussy," Kai groaned as he pushed in further.

Oh so slowly, he gave me inch after delicious inch of his cock, stretching me to the edge of my comfort zone. But I was made for my Mate and he was made for me so we fit perfectly. A deep moan came from me as he bottomed out, filling me with his amazing cock. He touched every pleasure spot inside of me, sparking pleasure with every move.

"Fuck, you feel amazing, Vanya," he whispered, savoring each slow withdrawal and gentle thrust.

"Oh, Goddess yes," I moaned as more pleasure filled me.

His pace increased, thrusting harder and faster into me. My pussy fluttered around his cock as if trying to keep him inside each time he pulled back. Every sensation felt heightened as if all of my nerve endings stood on high alert. I never imagined that being with my Mate could feel like this. Nothing could ever compare. Nothing would ever be so good as this.

"Mark me," I moaned as I could feel my orgasm coming near.

A low groan sounded from him while he fucked me harder. He leaned over, his whole body covering mine, and he licked a spot on my neck. A shiver of anticipation washed over me, knowing he was taking his time to find the perfect spot to claim me as his.

"So soft, so beautiful," Kai murmured as he nuzzled the spot on my neck. "All mine."

"Yes, all yours, forever," I said as goosebumps traveled from that spot over my body.

His hot breath fanned over the wet spot, and all of my attention was on him. His hand snaked around my front, circling my clit as he kept fucking me hard. Pleasure sparked, and I didn't think I could hold it back any longer, but I wanted his teeth in my neck.

"Come for me, my Mate," Kai purred.

The vibrations of his purr, mixed with the move of his hand and the thrusting of his cock, became too much for me. I came with a startled cry as pleasure washed over me. His teeth pierced my skin at the height of my pleasure and I screamed out. My whole body felt like it was on fire but in the best way. Warmth spread throughout my limbs, only enhancing my pleasure. Tremors racked my body as my pussy clenched around his cock and pleasure flowed through me. I could feel our mating bond connect, and his presence filled me with love.

When my body stopped trembling, Kai slowly pulled out. I whined at the loss, but he immediately turned me around, setting me in his lap.

"Your turn gorgeous. Ride me, mark me, claim me as yours," Kai said as he positioned me over his cock.

"Mine," I growled, feeling my wolf come to the surface.

I needed to claim my Mate so everyone would know that he was mine forever. His hands held me steady as I sunk down on his cock, loving the way he filled me to the brink. My pussy was sensitive, and I knew I could come again, but I wanted to focus on his pleasure now. I tightened my muscles around him, earning a strangled groan that sounded like music to my ears.

Leaning over, my naked breasts brushed against his chest as I looked for the perfect spot to mark him as mine. His hips pushed up, fucking me with short, shallow thrusts. When I licked the place where I would mark him, Kai moaned.

"Fuck, please, Vanya," he said as his hips moved faster, more urgently.

He wouldn't last much longer, and I wanted him to experience the same pleasure he had given me. As I squeezed my pussy around his cock, I pierced his skin with my teeth. With an earth-trembling growl, he came as our mating bond snapped into place. His pleasure flowed through me, igniting another climax. My pussy trembled around his cock as he filled me with his seed. We completed our mating, filling the small cabin with sounds of pleasure and sex.

Kai pulled me into his embrace, still connected in the most intimate ways. I loved his arms around me, his cock inside of me, and our mating bond alive and pulsing. Nothing could tear us apart now. Feeling safe and cherished, I fell asleep in his arms.

I woke up feeling heated, and horny reaching behind me to feel my strong mate cuddle me. With a low whine, I woke him up, and he immediately hugged me closer to him.

"What is wrong, my Mate? Tell me and I'll fix it," Kai said, leaning on an elbow so he could look at my face.

I could feel his hard cock poking in my ass and my pussy clenched achingly empty. My heat had suddenly started, probably ignited by our mating bond.

"You, now, please," I moaned.

He didn't waste a second and pulled one leg over his hip, opening me wide so he could easily slide inside of me. With a satisfied sigh, I closed my eyes as he filled my pussy with his cock.

"Fuck, you're hot and tight, and wet," Kai growled.

"I'm in heat," I moaned.

He held still, his cock trembling deep inside of me. "Does that mean we can make babies?" he asked.

I hadn't thought about the mechanics of two different shifter species mating, but my Heat showed me it should be possible. I arched my neck to look at him.

"Would you want that?" I asked.

A low purr came from him and spread around my body. I could feel his love fill me through our mating bond, and even before he said the words, I already knew the answer.

"More than anything in the world," Kai said.

"Then fuck me, breed me, fill me with babies, and make me a mama wolf," I moaned as my pussy squeezed around him.

His purr filled the cabin with a comforting sound as he pulled back and thrust inside of me again. His hips created a slow dance of seduction as one hand came around to play with my clit. Pleasure filled me with a steady beat.

This time, our lovemaking was slower and more relaxed as our mating bond connected us. We knew we had each other for the rest of our lives and he took his time to make pleasure fill every one of my senses.

When my orgasm washed over me, he immediately followed me behind, filling me with his seed, only enhancing my pleasure. Waves of pleasure washed over me as my body trembled and moans tumbled from my lips. My pussy milked his cock, squeezing every last drop of cum out of him until my pussy was overflowing. His groans of pleasure and the throbbing of his cock only enhanced my pleasure.

Our pleasure was one as our bodies came down from their highs. Kai pulled a blanket over us and kissed me. His presence grounded me and made me feel safe and cherished.

"I love you," my Mate said.

"I love you," I said.

Having the urge to nest had been a clear sign of the Moon Goddess that my Mate was close, and now that we were connected, I couldn't imagine my life without him.

THE END

Chased by the Gargoyle

After the most glowing recommendation from my best friend, I decided to go to the Monthly Human Monster Mixer. I was single and ready to mingle, but seeing all the different types of monsters surrounding me made me nervous. What if there was no one interested in chasing me?

I wasn't athletic, pretty, or bold enough to step up to some ferocious monster and ask them to fuck me. And my stutter made sure that even when I dared to open my mouth, nothing good came out of it. Just when I was considering calling it a night, the feeling of being watched washed over me. I've had that feeling so many times since I moved here, but now it is stronger than ever.

"Hi neighbor," a husky voice behind me said.

I turned around, and I came face to chest with a gorgeous Gargoyle I had never met before. "N... neighbor?" I asked.

"Yes. Don't you live in that attic space in the building on the corner of South Street?" he asked with a slow and seductive smile.

I nodded, not sure how this perfect specimen would know that or why he would pay attention to me. He was drop-dead gorgeous. His gray skin sparkled in the moonlight, and his white hair framing his face almost made it look like he was wearing a hallo. But the dark wings he spread wide and the way his black shirt stretched over his muscular arms were in no way angelic. Neither were my thoughts about him.

"I am in the penthouse across the street."

The penthouse across the street was the most impressive space I had ever seen. It had glass windows all around, and I had looked at it in envy from my small apartment, but I had never seen the owner before.

"Oh wow, the G... G... Graysons building?" I asked.

"Yes, that is mine," he said as he stretched out his hand. "William Grayson, a pleasure to meet you."

"Sadie," I mumbled as I grasped his hand.

It was colder and firmer than I had expected, but that was probably normal for a Gargoyle.

"Did you come here with anyone, Sadie?" he asked as he held my hand, and drew slow seductive circles on the back of it with his thumb.

"N... n... no," I stuttered, entranced by his presence so close to me.

"Me neither," William said as he took a step closer, almost enveloping me with his wings, so it felt like we were the only two people in the woods. "Have you done this before? Getting chased and fucked by a monster?"

I shook my head, sure that my voice would abandon me with his closeness. Everything around me evaporated as I looked into his brilliant amber eyes. They looked like liquid gold, swirling and mesmerizing me. How had I not seen him before? I was sure I would remember him.

William let go of my hand to cup my cheek, angling my head upwards. He bent down until our lips were only a hair's breadth apart. Arousal coursed through me, and my pussy clenched in anticipation. I could smell his breath and the tantalizing cologne that suited him so well.

"Would you like to be chased and fucked by me?" the gorgeous Gargoyle asked.

I moaned in response, my pussy quivering, achingly empty.

"I want to hear you say it, Sadie," he said, inching away when I leaned closer for a kiss.

"I... I... I want you to chase me an... and fuck me," I whispered.

As soon as the last word left my mouth, his lips descended onto mine. I moaned into the kiss, surprised by how supple his lips were underneath mine. They were cold and smooth like the finest marble, but they gave way with the press of my mouth. It didn't feel like kissing a statue; it felt like kissing a living monster.

His powerful arms and grand wings surrounded me, making this an intimate moment rather than a public one. I almost forgot where we were until he pulled back and all the sounds came rushing back to me.

"Let's go," William said as he pulled me towards the exit.

"B... but, weren't you going to ch... chase me?" I asked, my heart beating fast.

"Yes, but I know a much better place for it."

"Where?" I asked breathlessly.

"Do you trust me?" William asked.

I probably shouldn't, but I did. Maybe it was the familiar feel of his eyes on me or the way his kiss had made my world tumble upside down, but I wanted to see where this night would go.

With a nod, I sealed my fate. He pulled me out to the exit onto the entrance road, where there was enough room for him to spread his wings wide. He pulled me into his embrace and I lifted my head, hoping for another kiss.

With a gentle smile, he caressed my cheek and said. "Hold on tight."

Before I could understand what was going to happen, he used his massive wings to propel us and we soared up into the air. With a small squeal, I grabbed his shoulders tight. His powerful hands surrounded me, carrying me as if I weighed nothing. William was a tall but slim male, and I was considered on the bigger side of the scale, but he lifted me as if I was as light as a feather.

We flew over the trees, deeper into the dark forest. He covered acres of ground with just a few flaps of his wings. When we reached an open clearing deep into the forest where I couldn't even hear the commotion of the Monster-Human mixer, he landed.

William gently put my feet on the ground, but he never let go of me. His hands caressed my back, my ass, and my hips. Pleasurable shivers washed over me with his gentle touch. With slow and unsure movements, I let my own hands wander over his body. He moaned in pleasure when my hand reached the back of his neck and I caressed his sturdy white hair.

He pushed his hips against mine, and I could feel his hardness grow thicker. I moaned in response, as I could feel my pussy tremble in anticipation. I was achingly empty, and I really wanted him to fill me.

"Are you attached to this dress?" William asked as he dragged it up, revealing my naked thighs.

"Y... yes," I moaned.

I had worn one of my favorite dresses that hid my belly and accentuated my breasts in the hope it would give me enough confidence to approach someone.

"A shame," William rumbled as he lifted it higher. "I would have loved to rip it from your body. Next time you'll wear something I can tear off."

I moaned in response, my heart elated that he talked about a next time with me before this one was even over. I raised my arms so he could pull the dress over my head. My hands went to my back to undo my black bra, but he held me back.

"Leave it on," William rasped, as his eyes devoured me. "I love the color on your skin."

His hands cupped my breasts. They were plenty more than a handful, but he looked at them as if they were perfect. A soft moan escaped me as his thumbs caressed my nipples through the soft fabric.

"I could just watch you all day, Sadie. Pleasure on your face is the most beautiful thing in existence."

A blush washed into my cheeks, and I wanted to deny his statement, but a kiss made it impossible. His mouth devoured mine as his hands pleasured my breasts. A touch on my pussy startled me. I broke off the kiss with a gasp, looking in between us, seeing his tail push in between my legs. He groaned when it slipped inside my panties, discovering how wet I was for him.

"So slick and ready for me, Sadie."

I nodded, unable to utter another word as his hands and tail pleasured me. Each touch lifted me higher and higher, and I was so ready to fall with him on this dark night. His tail circled my clit and his hands worshiped my breasts as if I was the only thing in existence.

Before I could reach my climax, he turned me around. I could feel his rock-hard body behind me, his cock digging into my ass. One arm circled me, holding me flush against his body as his other pulled down my panties and removed his own pants. I wanted to look at him, but his hand held me steady.

His pants dropped down on the soft grass in a whisper. He bent his knees to push his cock in between my legs. I moaned when his cool, rock-hard cock touched my overheated pussy. I moved my hips slightly so he could slip inside of me, but he didn't. He teased me with slow and seductive thrusts in between my legs, coating his cock in my wetness, but never entering me.

A low whine escaped me, as I could feel the pleasure rise, but never crest. I needed more. I needed him inside of me, but I didn't dare ask, out of fear of losing him in this moment.

His mouth went to my ear, his cold breath fanning my face. He gently bit my earlobe, making a shiver wash over me and more arousal fill me. Just when I felt like I couldn't take it anymore, he whispered in my ear.

"Run."

It took a moment for my brain to catch up, but when his hands left me, it spurred me into action. I moved forward, almost tripping over a branch. The sounds of his wings behind me made me move faster, but I had only taken a few steps when he caught me.

"Fuck, your ass looks amazing when you run," William growled.

Before I could answer, he pushed me on my knees onto the soft grass. His massive body covered me and in one move, he was inside of me. I moaned when his amazing cock filled me, his length and girth stretching my pussy to fit him.

An earth-trembling growl sounded from him as he pulled back and thrust inside of me again. I had to hold myself steady as he fucked me from behind. His tail came around, circling my clit, sparking pleasure.

Sounds of pleasure left me as his hands gripped my hips tight, fucking me hard. My ass jiggled, and my tits swayed with each thrust as pleasure rose inside of me.

"Fuck, I love your legs, I love your ass, I love your pussy."

I moaned in response, not knowing how to answer his praise.

"I've watched you for so long, dreaming about having this ass underneath me," William growled as he thrust inside, his hands grabbing my ample ass firmly.

My arms were about to give out, but his words unlocked something inside of me. He had watched me? As if sensing my confusion, he pulled out and turned me around so I could face him. He lifted me up in his arms, impaling me on his cock again.

"Did you think it was a coincidence meeting each other here?" William asked, as his hips moved in a primal dance of seduction.

I shook my head as pleasure coursed through me, turning my brain to mush. His tail continued circling my clit, as if that was its sole purpose to exist.

"I followed you when I saw you leave your apartment tonight. I've been looking for an excuse to have you. Every night I flew by your windows, hearing your moans of pleasure. I had to hold myself back to not fly inside and give you my name to moan."

I moaned his name in response, overcome with pleasure and a warm feeling from his confession. He stood upright, his wings opening wide, taking in almost the entire width of the clearing in the forest. The movement caused his cock to sink into me even deeper, and I moaned in pleasure.

"All mine," William growled as he suddenly soared up into the sky.

My surprised scream turned into a moan of pleasure as the flap of his wings thrust his cock deeper inside of me. My legs wrapped around him on instinct and my hands gripped his shoulders tight as I watched him with my mouth wide open. I hadn't known what to expect from this chase, but his growled confession was certainly not it.

Pleasure flowed through me with each flap of his wings. Gravity and the movement of his body sunk his cock even deeper inside of me, hitting a spot I'd never found on my own before. Sounds I didn't recognize left me as pleasure rose steadily inside of me. William flew higher and higher, but there was never a moment of fear inside of me. I trusted him.

My pleasure grew, as did his movements. His tail came in between us, circling my clit, sparking even more pleasure. Each thrust and flap of his wings made a moan tumble from my throat. I've never had so much pleasure in such a short time. I usually took my time when I was masturbating. Slowly rose to the top, since I had a lot of trouble finishing with men, but with William, it all felt so natural. Before I even knew it, I could feel my orgasm begging to break free.

I looked into his amber eyes and all I could see was lust for me. No man had ever looked at me like that, but this Gargoyle did, for some reason.

"I... I... I'm..."

"Are you going to come for me, beautiful?" William asked as his tail sped up its movements.

I nodded. Too much pleasure flowed through me, and I needed to let it go. William fucked me harder, his eyes darkening and focusing on my face.

"Come for me, Sadie," William growled.

Somehow, those gravelly words were enough for me to let go. My orgasm flowed through me as my pussy squeezed around his rock-hard cock. He groaned in pleasure, my own pleasured cries mingling with his, lost in the wind. My nails dug into his hard shoulders, not even leaving a dent, as pleasure washed over me.

William slowed down his thrusts as he whispered sweet encouragements that intensified the pleasure coursing through me. His eyes never left mine while the last of my pleasure flowed out of my tired body.

"Can I take you home?" he asked as he gently laid my head on his shoulder.

"H... Home?" I asked.

"Yes, home. I want to fuck you in my bed on silken sheets like the queen that you are."

"Ok... Okay," I mumbled, burring my face into his chest.

He used his wings to fly higher, still buried inside of me. My pussy tightened around his cock, but I felt satisfied for the moment. He flew with sure and determined movements, holding me close to him. In no time at all, we were in the city. A blush crept up, realizing if anyone would look up, they would see my naked ass hanging out.

As if he could read my thoughts, William's hands cupped my ass, protecting me from any unsuspecting eyes. A few moments later, he landed on his gorgeous terrace overlooking the city with a soft thump. He moaned low as he slowly slid out of me and turned me around so I could look at the view. His arms surrounded me and he rested his chin on top of my head. My apartment might also be on the top of the building, but with the slanted roof and old windows that only looked up to the sky, I've never had a view like this.

"Beautiful," I sighed as I looked around at all the lights surrounding us.

"Just like you. You deserve everything beautiful in life, Sadie," William whispered in my ear.

Before I could answer, I felt his rock-hard cock poking against my ass. He led my hands to the railing and opened my legs with a soft push of his feet against mine. I followed his movements until I was bent over the railing overlooking the city and he pushed his cock inside of me again.

I moaned low as his amazing cock filled me again. The cold, soft texture of it, soothing my already abused pussy. At this angle, he touched other pleasure points than before, chasing my second orgasm of the night. His groans filled my senses as he fucked me from behind. His tail came out to play again, but it was careful of my sensitive clit. Each thrust built pressure inside of me, and I was already so close to bursting.

His hands gripped my ass firmly as he leaned back. With a strangled groan, he fucked me harder, making my ass bounce and my tits sway in the wind.

"Fuck, I love your ass so much," William groaned.

His tail slithered over my body until it was against my lips. With a moan, I opened my mouth, and it slipped inside. It tasted of a mix of me and him, a delicious, unique cocktail that I could only dream of recreating. When the tip was nice and wet, he pulled it out of my mouth. His hands pulled my ass cheeks apart as he kept fucking me. His tail circled around my puckered hole, sparking a different kind of pleasure.

"This ass is all mine," William growled as his tail dipped inside.

I moaned in agreement, ready to give him all of me. He pushed in just the tip, to give me a feeling of what it could be like. Pleasure sparked inside of me, and suddenly I burst. A cry of pleasure left me as my orgasm washed over me. My pussy squeezed around his cock as my legs trembled and almost gave out. My ass clenched around his tail as pleasure flowed through me. William groaned low while he left the tip of his tail inside and slowed down his thrusts. His powerful arms surrounded me as he pulled out his cock.

"I'll take this ass next time," William murmured in my ear as he lifted me up and carried me inside.

I moaned in response as my body still trembled from my release. He laid me on his massive bed on the softest sheets I've ever felt.

"I promised I would fuck you in my bed," William said.

I nodded, looking at his amazing cock for the first time. I could hardly believe that such a monstrosity had been inside of me. It didn't look like it would fit. He followed my gaze, grabbing his cock and stroking it slowly for me.

"You haven't…"

I couldn't finish the sentence without blushing, but he nodded.

"I haven't come yet. I can go all night for as long as I want. Do you want me to come inside of you?"

"Yes, please," I moaned, opening my legs and inviting him inside of me again.

I didn't know whose voice that belonged to. I sounded like a wanton woman, ready to be fucked by this gorgeous Gargoyle all night long.

William immediately crawled over to me, covering me with his massive body. His cock slipped inside of me easily, as if my pussy had already adapted to his size. He was heavy, and he pushed me into the soft bed, without smothering me. I couldn't move, but I loved his weight on top of me as he fucked me with slow movements of his hips.

"Fuck, you feel amazing, Sadie," William groaned.

It felt like he had all the time in the world, fucking me with slow and steady thrusts. My pleasure was building slowly, and I had time to look at him. His face was gorgeous, as if carved out by an artist with a love for their craft. I lifted my hand to cup his cheek, and he closed his eyes with a low moan.

After what seemed like forever, my big Gargoyle finally started to lose it. His body trembled and his moans came more frequently. His thrusts increased in speed, and I could feel his cock throb deep inside of me.

"Oh fuck, I'm going to come," William growled as he fucked me harder, sparking pleasure with each thrust.

"Yes, yes, yes," I moaned, overcome by my own pleasure.

I've come more times in one night than I had with any previous lover and I wanted him to come inside of me, fill me with his seed, and claim me as his. I squeezed my pussy around his cock, earning a strangled groan. He opened his eyes, looking at me with so much emotion, that my throat closed up.

"So, so good," William moaned.

His hips bucked, and he threw his head back, his entire body flexing and thrusting, on the verge of coming. It was the most beautiful thing I had ever seen, and I didn't want to miss a second of it.

He finally came with a strangled cry after giving me so much pleasure, and I followed his lead. A small orgasm sparked inside of me, making my pussy tremble around him, only enhancing his pleasure. His cock throbbed deep inside of me, filling me with his cum.

"Sadie," William groaned low as his body trembled with his release.

I whispered his name back as I caressed his cheek. His eyes focused on me again, and the most beautiful smile grazed his lips. William kissed me, slow and seductive, as if trying to keep me here without words, but he already had me.

I might have been looking for a fling at the Mixer, but I had found the most perfect Gargoyle and now that I had him, I would never let go.

THE END

If you enjoyed this story and want to read more stories about getting Chased by Monsters, check out Chased by the Werewolf[1], Chased by the Minotaur[2] and Chased by the Satyr[3]

---

1. https://books2read.com/u/bzKW7Z

2. https://books2read.com/u/m2qed1

3. https://books2read.com/u/mg5dwz

Saved by the Kraken

TW: Near drowning, loss of oxygen

There was something wrong. I knew I checked all of my equipment before diving but, there was something off with my oxygen level. I only noticed it when I was already too deep and too far away from the boat.

My heart was pounding, but I knew I had to stay calm. Black spots swam around my vision, and it wasn't the exotic fish I had been following.

Just before I lost consciousness, a massive blue, gray tentacle filled my view, and a strange sort of calmness came over me.

When I woke up again, I was in a damp cave filled with iridescent shells illuminating the stone walls. I've never seen anything more beautiful in my life. I wondered what type they were and where they came from. It looked like someone had taken a lot of time and attention to detail to create the gorgeous mosaic surrounding me.

A movement drew my attention, and I could scarcely hold in the gasp that bubbled up in my throat as a magnificent monster rose from the pool of water in the middle of the cave. Its skin was navy blue, his hair dark, and multiple gray tentacles surrounded him. A shiver washed over me as I could almost feel them on my skin. This must be the creature who saved my life and took me to his cave.

"What are you?" I asked, absolutely fascinated by his appearance.

I've seen many monsters in my lifetime and even dated a few, but I've never seen anything quite like him. His face was like a work of art, with a strong jawline, dark eyes, and supple lips. Even with his inhuman blue skin, he was a gorgeous specimen. The tentacles surrounding him entranced me with their color and mesmerizing movements.

"A Kraken," he rumbled, his delicious deep voice filling the cave and making shivers travel across my back. "We prefer to live in solitude, but you almost drowning right outside my cave disturbed my slumber."

"Thank you for saving me," I said, sure that I would have died without his help. "How can I repay this debt?"

He cocked his head as his tentacles emerged from around him, reaching for me. "I have always been fascinated by your kind," he said as he slowly inched closer, the sound of his slithering tentacles filling the cave. "What is your name, human?"

"Isla," I whispered, afraid that my voice was too loud for the intimate comfort of his cave.

"Hmm, like a piece of land surrounded by the sea?" he asked and I nodded. "My name is too difficult for your human tongue, so you may call me Jax."

"Jax," I said and his tentacles shivered, as if hearing his name on my tongue was pleasurable for him.

A shiver of anticipation washed over me as his eight tentacles slithered their way around me.

"You are so different from me," Jax said as he lifted a tentacle to touch my cheek.

The tentacle felt cold and wet against my skin, but not in an unpleasant way. The texture was rubbery, and I could see the suckers covering its length dilating.

"I am fascinated by the softness of your skin, your hair, your legs, and what treasures may lie in between them," the Kraken murmured as one tentacle touched my hair and another slithered over my naked calf.

I opened my legs on instinct, my pussy clenching and desire rising inside of me. The tentacle slowly slid higher across my calf as he leaned in closer. His musky, salty smell surrounded me as his black eyes burned bright with lust. His cute little nose crinkled as he sniffed at me.

"Your smell is... divine," Jax said.

Arousal coursed through me as wetness gathered between my legs. Could he smell my desire for him?

"Thank you," I said with a husky voice that didn't sound like my own.

"I know how you can repay your debt if you so please. I merely ask for just one taste of the treasure between your thighs."

"Yes, please," I moaned, feeling like I might die if I didn't feel his mouth on me.

It might be the oxygen deprivation or the near-death experience, but I've never wanted anything more than his tentacles on my body and his mouth on my pussy. Jax leaned in closer while his tentacle slid higher over my leg. His hands grabbed my thighs, spreading me wide as his other tentacles joined in as well, undressing me until I lay naked in front of this magnificent Kraken.

His mouth descended on my aching pussy and I moaned at the contact. He was colder than I had imagined, and it felt so good on my overheated pussy. The first lick of his tongue between my wet pussy lips made my back arch and a moan bubble up in my throat. The next lick was deeper, more urgent as if one taste wasn't enough. His tentacles held me steady as his tongue devoured me.

"Delicious," Jax growled.

He spread my legs wide, two tentacles slithering around them, applying a delicious amount of pressure on my skin. I could feel every single sucker attach itself to my skin, massaging my muscles. His tongue dove deep inside of my pussy as if trying to get to the source of my taste.

Pleasure rose inside of me as more tentacles focused on my upper body. Two of them surrounded my breasts, encompassing them like a makeshift bra as the tips circled my throbbing nipples. Two more gripped my arms, spreading me wide like an offering for this magnificent creature. I was completely at his mercy and I loved every second of it.

Another tentacle came around my throat with a heavy but comforting presence. He didn't apply any pressure. He was just there around my throat, holding my head up so I could look at what he was doing to my body. Tentacles surrounded me, pleasuring every inch of my body, but it wasn't enough.

"More, please," I moaned.

The Kraken lifted his head up, licking his shiny lips, his eyes half-lidded with desire. "You want more?" Jax asked.

His tentacles moved around my body, caressing my skin, pleasuring my nipples, making me feel unlike anything I ever experienced before. Pleasure was rising inside of me, but I needed more to reach my peak.

"Yes, please," I moaned, desperate for release.

"Tell me what you want," Jax growled as his hands tightened around my thighs in the same way his tentacles tightened around the rest of my body.

"My clit, please, lick, suck, do something to my clit," I moaned, my voice hoarse with desire.

His head dove down between my legs again, searching for that pleasure spot that would bring me to climax. His tongue licked me from back to front, and a small gasp escaped me when he ended at my clit. Jax rumbled happily, focusing on that spot, making me scream with pleasure. Now that he found my clit, it seemed as if he wouldn't rest until I was a moaning heap of pleasure.

The tentacles surrounding my body also moved with purpose. Two suckers attached themselves to my nipples, making me gasp with bliss. The slow, sucking sensation made pleasure rise inside of me.

His tongue circled around my pleasure spot, again and again, until it became too much and I burst. I screamed his name as pleasure flowed through me, my pussy clenching around nothing, achingly empty, while he surrounded my body with his tentacles. My body shivered and my pussy ached, restrained by his tentacles, somehow only increasing my pleasure.

"That was amazing," I moaned when his tongue left my sated pussy and he released his tight grip on my limbs.

I could feel the blood rushing through my veins as my pussy throbbed from my release.

"Yes," Jax rumbled as his black eyes focused on me. "But I am afraid that one taste will not be enough."

Before I could reply, he dove down between my legs again, aiming for my clit. A sound of shocked pleasure left me as he sucked on my clit, not letting up until he tore another orgasm from me. This one was unexpected, and quicker. My body trembled as my pussy clenched, and pleasure flowed through me. It was amazing, but I still wanted more of him.

"I need your cock," I sobbed, my pussy sated, but oh so empty.

"You need me to fill your empty pussy?" Jax growled.

"Yes, please, Jax," I moaned.

One of his tentacles appeared at my mouth, lightly tapping my lips. "Open," Jax growled.

I obeyed, and the tip of his tentacle slipped between my lips. I moaned at the salty taste on my tongue, already eager for more. Far too soon, he pulled it back, his tentacle now shiny with my saliva. He whisked it through the air over my body until it was at my weeping entrance. I wanted his cock, but a tentacle might just be the second-best thing.

Slowly but surely, he pushed it inside of my pussy. The texture was unlike anything I've ever experienced before. It wasn't hard like a cock, or soft like a tongue. It fell in between everything I knew. The squishy, cold feeling of it was unique and amazing, and I never wanted it to end.

The small tip slid in easily, barely stretching me, but the deeper he went, the wider his tentacle became. More and more of it filled my pussy, the tip coiling up inside of me to fit in more. Moans tumbled from my lips as the most amazing experience of being stretched and filled by him overtook my body. Jax pushed in deeper, the suckers lining his tentacle caressing the inside of my pussy, making pleasure fill my senses.

When I was as full as I could possibly be, he stilled, looking at my face. "Move, please," I moaned.

Jax growled in response, twisting the tentacle inside of me, caressing my pussy walls and sparking pleasure. Slowly, he pulled it out, only to thrust it back inside of me, making me dizzy with pleasure. Nothing has ever felt as good as this, and I opened my mouth to beg for more, but only sounds of pleasure left me.

It seemed as if he understood my wordless cry of pleasure, and refocused on my clit again. It was throbbing with my previous releases, but when he put one of his suckers on top of it, it came to life again. My climax broke to the surface as I was panting for air. Pleasure tore through me as his amazing tentacles stimulated my clit and pussy. My pussy squeezed around his squishy flesh, making the most obscene noises I've ever heard. My back arched, but I couldn't move with all of his tentacles surrounding me. I was immobile in the best way, just experiencing the pleasure he gave me.

His tentacle slid out of me, and I moaned at the loss, ready to beg for more, when another took its place. Jax repeated the same exact pattern with each of his eight tentacles, replacing them around my body. The small cave filled with the scent of my sweat and release as he wrung orgasm after orgasm from me.

"Beautiful treasure," his heavy voice rasped as Jax pulled out his last tentacle, making me feel achingly empty yet again.

"No more, please," I moaned, having come more in the last hour than in the last month.

"But you haven't had my cock yet."

"What?" I asked, delirious with pleasure, but aching to see and feel his cock.

I opened my eyes, that I must have closed along the way. Jax floated above me, supported by his tentacles, and I could finally see his cock. It looked like a mix between a cock and a tentacle. It was dark, long and thick, and I knew it would feel amazing in my abused pussy. As I looked at it, it suddenly moved just like one of his tentacles, curling and beckoning me closer. Oh, my dear lords, his cock was prehensile. I might not survive this, but if I didn't, I would die happily knowing I've experienced everything there is in this world.

"Do you want my cock inside of your pussy, Isla?" Jax asked, my eyes focused on the appendage.

I could only nod, as any rational thought left me, leaving me wordless. My lower body was still heavy with arousal, and desire burned bright inside of me.

"I need to hear you say it," Jax growled as his face came close to mine, filling my vision and breaking my gaze from his cock.

"What?" I asked, looking into his gorgeous black eyes.

"Do you want my cock?" Jax asked again, patiently, as if he had all the time in the world to fuck me.

I had no idea what time it was, or how long I had been in his cave, but it didn't matter, because I still needed his cock.

"Yes, I want your cock. Please, Jax, give it to me," I moaned, trying to widen my legs that were still surrounded by his tentacles.

"So beautiful, and needy," Jax murmured as he caressed my cheek with a finger. "I might keep you."

I didn't dwell on those words, as they might mean nothing more than just something he said during the height of our pleasure.

"Please fuck me," I groaned, ready to sleep for a week, but also desperate for his cock.

"With pleasure," Jax growled as he positioned my body on top of his tentacles in a shallow pool of water.

The cool texture on my back, and the cool water felt soothing against my overheated skin. His tentacles slithered away from my limbs, only supporting my body as he positioned his cock at my entrance. My body and pussy felt used in the best way, and I was ready to receive the last of him.

Slowly, Jax pushed his cock inside my pussy. He was big, and I was grateful for his tentacles, preparing me for this massive intrusion. Inch after delicious inch he gave me, stretching my pussy to take all of him. It felt like it would be too much, but it felt too good to tell him to stop.

"Jax," I moaned his name as pleasure filled me.

"My treasure," he replied, his voice strained as if he was trying to hold himself back.

I didn't want him to hold back. I wanted all of him. I've already experienced more pleasure than I ever had and I wanted to give something in return.

"You feel so good inside of me," I moaned. "So full, so right, so good."

A full-body shiver washed over him, and I could feel him tremble all around me. His cock twitched inside of me, and my pussy squeezed around it in response.

"You are so tight around me. So hot, and pulsing," Jax groaned.

"Yes, now please move."

Jax pulled out, making me whimper with the loss of his thickness inside of me, but before I could beg, he pushed back in, filling me all over again. Sounds of pleasure tumbled from my lips as he repeated the movement again, and again, fucking me hard on top of his writhing tentacles.

His cock felt amazing inside of me. His flesh was soft, but unwavering as it filled me with so much more than I've ever experienced before. Just as I wanted to ask how it moved before, he moved it inside of me on a downward thrust. My mind exploded with the sensation of his cock searching for a spot inside of me that only increased my pleasure. When his cock found it and he flicked over it, my legs seized up and a garbled sound left me.

"Yes," Jax growled, as he thrust inside of me again, repeating the movement with his cock. "Just like that. Come for me, my treasure. Squeeze my cock."

All I could do was obey his command. My orgasm washed over me as his cock filled me again and again. I could feel him throb deep inside of me, massaging that spot over and over again until pleasure consumed me. My pussy squeezed around his squishy flesh, milking him of his own release. With an earth-trembling growl, Jax came, stuffing my pussy full with his cum.

It was too much for me to hold, and I could feel it trickling out around his cock, being washed away by the water. A sense of loss filled me as his cum left me, my pussy desperate for more, even though I didn't think I could survive much more of him. Pleasure took over my senses as my body trembled with my release. I lost count of the number of orgasms I had experienced, but they all blanked into comparison with this all-consuming feel of pleasure and release.

As I slowly came down from my incredible high, I could feel his chest against mine, his heart beating fast. I felt connected to him, with his cock still inside of me and his tentacles surrounding me. Jax caressed me with his hands and tentacles, easing me down from the best orgasm in my life.

"I think I finally found a reason to leave my cave," Jax murmured against my hair, his arms and tentacles tightening around me.

"Yeah, what?" I asked, almost on the edge of sleep, but curious about his answer.

"You, my treasure," Jax said, kissing the top of my head. "Now sleep. You need your rest for what else I have in mind for you."

A shiver of delight washed over me as I fell asleep in the Kraken's embrace that had saved my life.

———— ❧ ————

THE END

———— ❧ ————

If you love tentacles and want more, check out my Japanese Kraken Bathing with the Akkorokamui[1]

---

1. https://books2read.com/u/3LVqEX

Interviewing the Yeti

This was going to be the interview of my career. The Yeti clan was notoriously private, and no one knew about their customs, only that in recent years human women had come, mated, and stayed, raising cute half-yeti babies together.

I've read almost every book about Yetis I could find, but besides some vague local legends, there truly was very little known about this type of monster. Excitement coursed through me, knowing this interview was going to be groundbreaking. I still couldn't believe I managed to get the clearance and approval of the Yeti Clan leader.

Trent the Yeti met me at the bus stop, and I was in awe at how enormous he was. I had seen photos and read about them, but seeing a massive Yeti in real life was a different story altogether.

"Hi," I piped up at the gorgeous Yeti Clan Leader, and he smiled warmly back at me.

His piercing blue eyes framed by his white fur were stunning, and I couldn't help myself getting lost in them. No, focus Charlotte, you came for an interview not to climb his bones.

"Welcome, Charlotte," Trent said, and his deep voice seemed to rumble right through me.

I suddenly wished we were doing a podcast interview so other people could hear his amazing voice, but that would have been even more difficult to arrange.

"Thank you," I said.

Trent motioned to the sled he had brought, and I sat on it. The trip up the mountain was brutal for untrained hikers, and being a city girl through and through, I was grateful for the sled. The wind blew around us, and whenever I tried to ask him a question, the wind took it away. I gave up trying to talk to Trent and focused on taking notes, but my fingers were so cold, I could hardly hold my pencil.

Putting my material away, I looked at my surroundings and gasped. We had left civilization behind and beautiful mountains and snow stretched as far as the eye could see around us. Without Trent, I would have never known which way to go and would have been lost in minutes. But the big Yeti seemed to see the way, even though everything looked the same in my eyes.

After what seemed like an eternity and made the chill settle in my bones, we arrived at a clearing surrounded by caves. Squinting, I could make out several dots walking around, and I realized it must be the Yeti village. Excitement coursed through me as I watched the figures grow as we came closer. There were so many more Yetis than I had imagined. I thought there were a handful, but looking around, I could see over twenty figures of different sizes walking around.

In the middle of the clearing was a big fire burning with a massive pot on top of it, with something that smelled so good that my stomach growled in response.

Trent looked behind him and smiled. "Want to taste?" he asked.

His rumbled words did things to my insides that had nothing to do with food, but I knew he meant the soup and not him, so I nodded.

"That would be lovely, thanks," I said.

He got me a bowl while introducing me to the people surrounding the fire. There were five Yetis and two human women. Seeing them stand next to each other, I couldn't imagine how that would ever work sexually, but considering a half-yeti child suddenly ran up to one of the human women, screaming mama, mama, it probably did.

I should write notes and take pictures, but my fingers were still too numb to hold anything. Trent gave me a bowl of soup, and I could feel the warmth seep into my hands, and my fingers tingle with the change in temperature. The smell was amazing, and when I took a tentative sip, I groaned in pleasure as the delicious taste exploded in my mouth.

Trent looked at me with his gorgeous blue piercing eyes and I could feel myself heat up from the inside out. The focus of my interview had been the interspecies couples and children, but I couldn't keep my eyes off the Yeti leader. I wanted to get to know him more, ask him all kinds of questions, and maybe discover if his white fur was as soft as it looked.

When I finished my soup, I asked to see his home, so I could warm up and write some notes down.

"I will gladly welcome you in my cave," Trent said with a nod, extending his hand to me.

I wouldn't mind welcoming him into my cave, but I couldn't say that, so I just bit my lip and nodded. It was a short track up the slope, and when I turned around just in front of the entrance of the cave, I could see why he had picked this one. It overlooked the valley and you could see everyone in almost one glance.

"What a gorgeous view," I sighed.

"It is," Trent said, looking at me.

Heat crawled up my cheeks as I felt his eyes on me. I wanted to be bold, but my courage left me as soon as I looked up and got lost in his gorgeous blue eyes. An interviewer losing her words was like a surgeon losing their scalpel. I felt naked and seen by him in a way I hadn't felt before, as if he stared through my facade right into my heart.

When a cold gust of wind made me shiver, Trent broke eye contact and ushered me into his cave. It was smaller than I had imagined, considering he was the clan leader. It was scarcely bigger than my one-bedroom apartment in the city, but much cozier. In the middle, a fire burned, casting a warm glow on the stones surrounding us. Lush furs covered the floor and the bed that stood to the side, making it all look very inviting.

"You will be warm here," Trent said as he threw another log on the fire.

"Thank you," I said as I went closer to the flames.

I shook off my coat and pulled off my gloves to dry them in front of the fire. When I felt like I could move my fingers without the tingling, I pulled out my notebook and recorder.

"Do you mind if we get started? I was hoping to get back in time for the last bus."

Trent shook his head. "You will have to stay the night. The wind is picking up, and a storm is coming. Even if we leave now, we will be stuck in it, and it is not safe for you."

"Oh," I said, blinking rapidly. "I hadn't realized it would be such a long journey, and I haven't brought anything to sleep in."

"One of the human females will have something you can lend for the night," Trent said, as if it wasn't an issue.

"Oh, okay. That means I will have more time to interview everyone," I said with a shrug.

Trent nodded and sat down next to me on the furs. His nearness made me flush, and I could feel him radiate body heat. I wouldn't mind snuggling up to him at night, but I shook the thought out of my head.

We started the interview and Trent answered each question with his rich voice. I already knew I would be listening to the interview tape again and again just to hear his delicious rumble. When he talked about the mated couples, my curiosity got the better of me.

"How come you are still single?" I blurted out.

Trent stiffened and averted his eyes, and I immediately felt guilty for bringing it up.

"I'm so sorry. Forget I asked. That was super inappropriate of me," I said, scratching my pencil on the paper to distract myself and avoid looking at him.

Trent grabbed my hand, turning to me, and making me look at him. "I have yet to find a female who wants to be with me."

I gaped at him in disbelief. This gorgeous Yeti couldn't find a date? What had this world gone to?

"How? You are gorgeous. Walk around in the city and women will throw themselves at your feet," I said, not adding I would gladly be one of them.

"That is part of the issue. I need to stay here with my clan. They count on me. I cannot go to the city to find a female when I have business to attend to here. Why are you still single if the city is so full of people?" Trent asked as his thumb drew lazy circles on the back of my hand.

A shiver washed over me as I imagined his warm hands in other places of my body.

"I haven't found the right man or monster yet," I said, my voice hoarse.

"And what would be the right monster for you?" the big Yeti asked as his voice turned sultry. "What do you look for in a monster?"

I noted with a shiver that he totally ignored the man's part of my words. I glanced up and got lost in his piercing blue eyes.

"Well, I like someone tall," I said.

Being a tall girl myself, I loved having someone tower over me, making me feel small and feminine. Trent nodded and leaned in closer, crowding my body, and giving me that feeling I craved.

"I'm a sucker for piercing blue eyes," I said as he came even closer.

On instinct, I leaned back until I was lying on the furs and he was hovering over me.

"What else?" Trent asked, his voice hoarse with desire.

His lips were impossible to ignore, drawing my gaze down instantly. His mouth was full and free of the white fur covering the rest of his face.

"I really like kissing, so he would need to be a good kisser," I whispered as his mouth came closer.

"Can I kiss you, Charlotte?" Trent asked so sweetly I couldn't say no, even if I wanted to.

"Yes, please," I moaned, and his mouth covered mine.

Sparks flew between us as our lips touched. His mouth was warm and soft against mine, and I moaned as his hands caressed my body. Trent took advantage of the sound I made to slip his tongue between my lips, searching for mine. His taste exploded in my mouth as my tongue played with his. He tasted like a mix of smoked brandy, pine trees, and pure sex.

My hands went to his head, touching the fur that felt so much softer than I had imagined. He groaned against my mouth as his hands roved over my sides to my breasts. I arched into his touch, my breasts heavy with desire. His mouth left mine to trace his lips over my cheek to my neck.

"Can I taste you, Charlotte?" Trent asked.

"Oh Gods, yes, you can taste me anywhere you want," I moaned.

He growled low, making a shiver wash over me, but it wasn't in fear, it was in desire. Trent's hands pulled at my clothes, and I helped him expose my breasts. His mouth closed over one of my nipples and I gasped as pleasure pulsed through me.

"Gods, yes, that feels so good," I moaned.

Trent rumbled in response, making vibrations course through me. My empty pussy clenched around nothing, producing wetness, achingly empty. When he was happy with the treatment of my first nipple, he switched breasts, sucking the other one into his mouth.

My back arched off the bed as pleasure flowed through me. I've always had sensitive breasts, and I loved nipple play, but not all my partners had been into it. It seemed as if Trent knew what I needed without me even having to say the words out loud.

He let my nipple go with a plop, his piercing eyes burning bright with desire. His fingers closed around my nipples, gently pinching them until I gasped. He mastered the perfect amount of pressure that made me balance that sweet line between pleasure and pain. They throbbed between his fingertips as pleasure flowed from my nipples to my pussy.

"Can I taste more of you, Charlotte?" he asked, and I loved my name on his lips.

"Yes, please, my pussy is aching," I moaned, as I lifted my hips up to pull my pants down.

I needed his mouth on my pussy almost as much as I needed my next breath. Trent smiled and kissed his way down over my stomach to between my thighs. I had to open them wide to accommodate his wide shoulders, and I loved the tickle of his soft fur against the inside of my legs.

Trent inhaled, groaning as he smelled my arousal. His tongue slid from his mouth, and I could see the pink monstrosity dive down between my pussy lips. I moaned as his massive, wet tongue touched my aching pussy.

"So wet," he growled against my pussy, and I moaned in reply.

His fingers were still around my nipples, pulling and teasing as his tongue lapped between my pussy lips. He was taking his time discovering every inch of my wet pussy with his amazing tongue. When he licked my clit, I groaned and my back arched off the soft fur involuntarily. Trent seemed to enjoy making me react because he repeated the motion over and over again until I could feel I was so close to coming I might burst.

"Please, Trent. I'm going to... going to... come," I gasped as his tongue didn't let up his assault on my clit.

He growled low and only doubled his efforts, pinching my nipples harder as he lapped at my clit. My hands were in his fur, tugging and pulling, but he kept going.

"Oh, Gods, Trent, yes," I moaned as I could feel my pleasure reach its peak.

My orgasm washed over me, and I could feel my whole body tremble with pleasure. More wetness flowed from my pussy and Trent lapped it up, groaning in delight. I cupped my breasts, and he gently released my nipples, making my climax only more intense. My pussy clenched around nothing, achingly empty, desperate to be filled.

"Fuck me, please," I moaned as the last of the tremors of my orgasm left my body.

It had been a mind-blowing climax, but I wanted more. I ached to be filled by him, and feel his cum inside of me. I didn't know where all these lustful thoughts had come from, but I embraced them wholeheartedly.

"You know Yetis breed for life, Charlotte," Trent said as he came up from between my thighs, his lips shiny with my wetness.

"Yes, take me, fuck me, breed me," I moaned.

"Do you want to stay here and let me fuck that sweet pussy every day until you become swollen with child? Do you want me to breed you, and fill you with my seed?" Trent growled as he loomed over me again.

He might seem frightening at that moment, but I knew it came from something primal inside of him, and I realized I wanted all of it. I wanted him to breed me and fill me with Yeti babies. Coming here for an interview that could change my career, I found myself inexplicably drawn to the idea of the Yeti clan leader claiming me as his. I could still work remotely, write articles about the Yeti way of life, and maybe even help the other Yetis find partners as I had found Trent.

"Yes, Trent. Breed me. Make me yours," I said as I grabbed his shoulders and pulled him towards me.

Our mouths met in a kiss filled with passion. I could taste myself on his lips, and I loved our tastes mingled together. He groaned against my mouth, pulling my legs around his waist, and I could feel his erection against my wet pussy. It felt unseemly big, but I knew it would fit. He dragged his erection through my juices, coating him in my wetness to ease the way.

As he positioned his cock at my entrance, he broke the kiss, panting. "Are you sure?" Trent asked for the last time, and I admired his inner strength.

He was so close to fucking me and was still concerned about my well-being. I pushed up my hips, letting his cock head slip inside of me, stretching me.

"Yes, fuck me now, Trent," I groaned.

His whole body trembled, but he took my words and pushed inside of me. His massive cock stretched my pussy to fit him, making me moan with pleasure. I've never had anything as big as him inside of me, but it felt so good I knew he ruined me for any other man or monster in the future.

"So good, so big," I moaned.

"You're so tight, Charlotte," he groaned, pulling back and thrusting back inside of me, giving me even more of his cock.

I looked down between us and saw that only half of him was inside, and I already felt so full.

"Give me all of it," I groaned. "Give me your cock, and breed me."

Trent growled low, pulling out again and thrusting even further inside of me. Thrust after thrust gave me more of his delicious cock until he bottomed out in my pussy and I could feel his cock so deep I could almost taste him.

"Yes, now fuck me, fill me with your cum," I said, trying to move my hips, but I couldn't move his massive body on top of me.

Trent looked at me with half-lidded eyes filled with lust and something more. Before I could try to identify it, he grabbed my hips and truly started to fuck me. Thoughts flew from my head as if they were birds scared by a sudden sound, and all I could do was feel. I felt his massive body on top of me, his amazing cock filling me, and his fur tickling me. The sensations were too much, and pleasure flowed through me. My pussy clenched around his cock as if trying to keep him inside of me as he fucked me with sure and deep strokes.

Sounds left me I've never even made before, as his cock did things to me I've only dreamed of. I couldn't even describe the feeling on paper if I wanted to. It was too much, too good, too much pleasure flowed through me, making everything around me disappear.

Trent groaned on top of me, and I could feel his cock throb deep inside of me, signaling his impending release. I wanted to come with him and milk his cock of his seed. I pushed a hand between us, flicking a finger over my clit, and in moments my orgasm washed over me.

I screamed his name as pleasure washed over me, and my pussy clenched around his cock. Trent emitted a hoarse cry of joy as he came as well, filling me with his cum. His seed spurted out of his cock as pleasure flowed through me, my pussy greedily milking him of all of it.

With a groan, he pulled out and rolled off me on the furs, pulling me in his arms. I snuggled against his soft fur, my body still trembling with pleasure.

"Mine," Trent murmured as he caressed my cheek with one of his meaty fingers.

"Yes, and you're mine as well," I said as I licked at his finger, loving the way his eyes burned bright with lust again.

I couldn't wait to do that again, and again, but my body needed to come back from that amazing high for a moment. This might not have been the interview that changed my career, but it was the one that changed my life.

THE END

If you enjoyed this story and want to read about more Yetis breeding their mates check out:

Saved by the Yeti[1], Trapped with the Yeti[2], Waking the Yeti[3] and On a Date with the Yeti[4]

---

1. https://books2read.com/u/bQj7VP

2. https://books2read.com/u/bopvPZ

3. https://books2read.com/u/bxNkYD

4. https://books2read.com/u/4jYqrD

Meeting with my Mate

My Mate was balls deep inside of me, and it felt so good I wanted to scream. But I couldn't make a sound, because no one knew what we were doing. This was such an important meeting, and I should pay attention. I had worked hard to plan this meeting with all the different parties, but his cock just felt too good inside of me.

I wanted to look behind me to see the face of the man that was giving me so much pleasure without even moving, but I couldn't. It almost felt as if I was frozen and observing what was happening from a faraway perspective while still feeling his cock deep in my pussy. I tried to lift a finger, but my body wasn't listening to me. My pussy squeezed around his cock, and I could feel it throb inside of me, making pleasure bloom, but I needed more to come, so much more.

A man on the other side of the table said something, and I tried to focus on his face, but it remained blurry. The man behind me chuckled and his cock jostled inside of me, making me moan. Everyone around the table froze, including the male buried in my pussy.

"Everybody, out, now," he growled, his voice deep and rough like an animal.

His voice sounded familiar, and yet I was sure I'd never heard it before. Everyone immediately obeyed and in seconds, the meeting room was empty.

"Are you a needy little Mate?" the voice asked, and I moaned instinctively in response.

Mate? I knew what that word meant in the shifter circles, but I didn't have a Mate. I didn't even have a boyfriend, but the man didn't seem to care. He stood up with his cock still buried inside of me and gently lay me face down on the table. He pulled out slowly, making me feel every inch of his cock as he dragged it out of my tight channel. It felt so good that every question or concern in my mind just evaporated.

"Your pussy is so wet and hot I had to hold back from shooting my load inside of you," he groaned.

I moaned as he pushed back inside, sparking pleasure deep inside of me as he filled my pussy like it had never been filled before. The sounds he made only enhanced my pleasure. He sounded like a man on the edge of sanity as if he had to do everything in his power not to ravish me and flood my pussy with his seed. I could feel his cock throb inside of me, and I craved his cum. My pussy clenched around his length, earning me a strangled groan of pleasure from him.

"Yes, squeeze me tight, my little Mate."

I wanted to come; I needed to come, and I needed him to come inside of me. Pleasure rose with every thrust of his cock, and moans tumbled from my lips. I've never been so quick, so close to a climax before. As his groans grew wilder and more animalistic, I could feel it rising within me. I wondered what kind of shifter he was.

"Are you going to come around my cock?" he asked, but I needed something more to reach that height.

As if he read my mind, he let his hand slip around me, finding my throbbing clit. He circled it gently, sparking a deep kind of pleasure. I was rushing towards my climax so fast, I could almost taste it. My pussy clenched around his cock as he fucked me harder and faster while fingering my clit. So, so close, I was almost-

Piep, piep, piep.

My alarm clock woke me from the most vivid sexual dream I had ever had. I moaned as I pushed my hand between my legs, finding my pussy soaking wet and throbbing, desperate for a release. Looking up at the clock, I froze. I was late for my meeting. How had that happened? I was sure I had set my alarm early enough for me to shower and get dressed, but the numbers on the little screen didn't lie.

With a curse, I flew out of bed and pulled on the clothes I had readied yesterday. No shower, and no orgasm for me this morning. I sprayed some deodorant and dabbed a few drops of perfume before running out to catch a taxi for my meeting.

My body was humming with unfulfilled pleasure and my pussy was aching and wet. I hoped the meeting would go smoothly so I could go home and grab my vibrator to relieve that amazing dream again.

As soon as I entered the conference room, I gasped as recognition washed over me. It was the same room I had dreamed about. The man at the head of the table lifted his head, and when our eyes met, I could feel a zing pass through my body straight to my throbbing clit.

"Everybody, out, now," he growled.

A shiver washed over me as I recognized his voice from my dream. Could this be... my Mate? I didn't even notice everyone leaving. I walked over to him as if pulled by an invisible thread. He stood up, towering high above me that even with my heels I had to crane my neck to look at him.

The man was gorgeous, dressed in a well-tailored suit that hugged his muscular arms. He had brown hair swiped up in a casual style, neatly trimmed stubble covering his chin and cheeks that I just knew would feel heavenly on my skin, and piercing blue eyes that seemed to look right into my soul.

"Hello, little Mate," he rumbled. "I dreamed about you last night."

"I did too," I whispered, suddenly feeling like my voice was too loud for the intimacy of this moment.

"What's your name, gorgeous?" he asked as he lifted his hand to cup my cheek.

"Scarlett," I said, and he caressed my bottom lip with his thumb.

"I'm Shane. Scream it when you come," he said as he bent down and kissed me.

His lips on mine were soft but demanding at the same time. He took charge of the kiss, gently nipping at my lips until I opened up to let his tongue inside. I moaned when his taste filled my senses. He tasted like coffee and smoked brandy, two of my favorite things mixed together.

His tongue met mine in a slow dance of seduction as his hands roved over my body. Shane was wrinkling my perfectly ironed clothes, but I didn't care until he grabbed my pants with the intention of ripping them off.

I broke the kiss, panting as I covered his hands with mine.

"This is my favorite pair of trousers. I don't care if you are my Mate, I will cut you," I said, my voice so breathless it probably didn't have the desired effect, but Shane listened.

"Feisty little Mate, I like it," he said as his hands went to the fastening of my pants, and unbuttoned it slowly. "So you are the Scarlett I am negotiating with today? I am just saying that as soon as these pants come off, you can get everything you want from me, sweetheart."

I gasped as he pushed a hand inside of my pants, discovering my aching pussy and the wetness in my panties. He pulled back, groaning as he licked his hand.

"So wet for me," Shane said as he pulled my pants down. "I can't wait to taste this sweet pussy."

My pumps fell to the ground with a resounding clonk, and my pants followed in moments. My lace panties were almost translucent with how wet I was, and he groaned in appreciation.

"By the Moon Goddess, you are gorgeous," Shane said before he dove down between my thighs, licking me over the wet fabric of my panties.

In response, I let out a moan, aware that I should probably speak up more, maybe even protest a little, but the pleasure was too intense, and it felt as though we were meant to be together. I put aside my common sense and all the questions I had and just enjoyed how his amazing tongue felt on my aching pussy. It would seem I would get my morning orgasm after all.

"Oh Gods, Shane," I moaned, and he rumbled happily in reply.

He licked me like a man parched as if he hadn't had a drink in ages, and my pussy was a direct source of his relief. He pulled my panties to the side as if he needed more of my taste and I moaned as his tongue made direct contact with my pussy. His tongue dove deeper, licking me in between my pussy lips and encountering my clit. My pussy clenched, producing even more wetness as he licked my clit and focused his attention on it. In moments, I felt like I would shatter, and Shane just kept going, intent on making me come.

I moaned his name on repeat like a prayer and he only increased his attention. His mouth, lips, and tongue were doing things to me I couldn't even put into words. His lips suctioned over my clit and as he applied just the right amount of pressure, the climax washed over me. I screamed his name as pleasure filled my senses. My pussy clenched around nothing, achingly empty, as he gently sucked on my clit. My body trembled as pleasure washed over me, and my mind went blank.

Shane happily lapped up my juices as I was trembling from the force of my orgasm. I enjoyed coming as much as the next girl, but I've never come so fast and so hard with a new partner before.

"Goddess, I could stay between your legs for the rest of my days, and die a fortunate man," he growled as he lapped up my release.

I moaned as the last tremors of my climax left my body. When the haze of pleasure slowly disappeared, I realized what we had done. People were on the other side of that door and I had to come back from this meeting with a victory or my company would fire me.

I sat up, attempting to pull my shirt down to try to cover my naked pussy.

"We shouldn't have-," Shane broke me off with his lips on mine, and I moaned into the kiss.

His taste mingled with mine, and his tongue plundered my mouth, making the protests disappear. He pulled back, caressing my cheek, and looking into my eyes with so many emotions I had to look away for a moment.

"There is so much more I want to do to you, my Mate. This was only the beginning."

"But the negotiations," I said.

"I don't care about those. I'll pay whatever is needed to solidify the deal, and I want you to come to work with me."

"You- what?" I asked, looking back at him. "You can't just offer me a job because I'm your Mate."

"The fact that you are my Mate is only a bonus, sweetheart. I was planning on offering it to you before I even saw you," he said as he pulled out a contract from his suitcase. "I've never met a better negotiator than you. I'll pay you double what you are getting now."

I accepted the papers and glanced them over. Knowing that he admired me so much that he wanted to poach me made me feel warm inside.

"So if I were to accept this job offer, would being your Mate have nothing to do with it?"

"Nothing," Shane said as he caressed my naked legs. "Consider it a bonus. I'll get you the office next to mine, so whenever you need me, I'll be there to service you."

I hooked my feet behind his legs and pulled him closer to me until his body was flush against mine. His rock-hard cock was still trapped inside his pants, and I could feel it throb, begging to be let out.

"What if I needed to be serviced now?" I asked, pulling his head down for another kiss and throwing the contract behind me.

"Your wish is my command, my Mate," he growled as he plundered my mouth.

His tongue met mine in a fiery dance of passion as I pulled at his pants, trying to get them off. My pussy was achingly empty, and I needed his cock to fill me. Shane helped me and in moments, I had his rock-hard, throbbing cock in my hands. I broke the kiss, needing to look at him, and I gasped as I saw how big he was. I caressed him from tip to bottom and moaned as I realized my fingers couldn't meet around the base where he was wider.

"Is that..."

"My knot. Yes," Shane groaned.

I've heard about them, but I've never seen a shifter cock up close and personal. I knew there were all kinds of toys, but it had never attracted me before. Holding it in my hand now, feeling it throb with need, made me want nothing else for the rest of my life.

"What kind of shifter are you?" I asked as I caressed his cock again slowly.

"Wolf," Shane gritted out between his teeth. "Goddess, if you keep stroking me like that, I might embarrass myself."

"That would be a shame," I said with a smile. "Because I really want your cock deep inside of me as you cum."

I loved how he was trembling under my touch and how my words made him groan.

"Condom?" Shane asked.

"I don't have any, but I am on the pill."

"I'm afraid that won't work when I mark you," Shane groaned as I caressed his cock again.

I was so mesmerized by his throbbing appendage, that his words almost didn't register. "Mark me?" I asked.

"I'll bite your neck when we both cum to show everyone I have claimed you, but I'm pretty sure that transcends birth control."

"Just give me the tip then, and pull out when you cum."

Shane shook his head. "My knot will ensure I can't pull back when I cum."

"Oh," I said, looking at the big bulge at the root of his cock. "Will it get even bigger?"

"Yes, but my bite will help you. You'll heal faster and stretch to take my knot."

"So you'll fuck me. Make me cum. Bite me. Fill me with your seed and push that big knot inside of me so none goes to waste?" I asked, my voice hoarse with desire.

My pussy clenched as if ready to receive all that he had to give. I was ready for him, our mating bond, and any children that may follow from it.

"Goddess, help me," Shane said, closing his eyes for a moment. When he opened them, I could see another color flash through the blue, and I knew it was his wolf coming to the surface. "Yes, my sweet Mate. I'll do all those things, but I'll make you cum again and again and I'll flood that pussy with so much seed it will surely take root and you'll be filled with my pups in no time," his voice sounded deeper, more hoarse as if he was on the edge of his control.

A shiver of desire washed over me, and I didn't want to wait another second to feel his cock inside of my achingly empty pussy. Finding my Mate today had been a surprise, but I was ready to have someone to share my life with and to love unconditionally.

"Yes, Shane. Mark me, Mate me, Breed me," I moaned as I pulled him towards me.

His cock touched my weeping entrance, and I gasped as he slowly pushed inside of me. He was too big, too good, too perfect. Pleasure bloomed inside of me as he entered my tight channel. His cock was made for my pussy, stretching me to my limit as he pushed more and more of him inside.

"So tight, and hot, and wet," Shane groaned as he gave me inch after delicious inch of his cock.

"More," I moaned, eager to get all of it inside.

"Needy little Mate," he groaned as he pushed in further, finally bottoming out inside of me.

"I need your knot," I moaned, knowing he still had more to give.

"You need to relax a bit before you can take it," Shane said, and pushed his hand between us, stroking my clit and making pleasure spark.

My pussy tightened around him, making us both groan with pleasure. He slowly pulled back and thrust inside of me again. His cock was so big, and I was so tight, he could barely move. As he played with my clit, my pussy relaxed a bit and he could fuck me harder. I wanted more; I needed more, but the words left me as the pleasure started to rise inside of me.

"My gorgeous Mate," he groaned as he fucked me faster and I could feel my orgasm rise.

"Yes, Shane, my Mate," I moaned.

It seemed my words ignited something inside of him because he started to fuck me like a madman. The giant table I was lying on scraped over the floor with the force of his thrusts, and all I could do was just lay here and take it like a good little Mate. Pleasure rose inside of me with each thrust and each flick over my clit. In moments, it became too much, and my orgasm took over.

"Mine," Shane growled as his cock throbbed deep inside of me.

I screamed his name as pleasure washed over me and my pussy clenched around his cock. He groaned, leaning over me, and putting his mouth on my neck.

"Yes, mark me, make me yours," I moaned when I felt him hesitate.

His teeth pierced my skin, and it felt like my orgasm was magnified. A mixture of pain and pleasure flooded my senses and my pussy opened up for him. After a few more thrusts, I could feel him enter more, and his big knot stretched me to my limits. I bucked up against his hips, trying to get it all inside of me. The sounds of our pleasure were mixed, and I could almost taste his desire.

"So good, such a tight little pussy," Shane growled against my neck, licking the skin he had pierced.

He moved his hips slightly, pushing the big knot even deeper, and when my pussy clenched around it, he came with a strangled groan. His knot swelled as his cock throbbed and he gave me all of him. His cum flooded my pussy and even more pleasure filled me as he claimed me as his.

"Goddess, you take my knot so beautifully. I'm gonna stay inside of this tight pussy forever," he groaned.

I've never had so much pleasure in such a short time, and my mind became mush. My pussy milked his cock, trying to get all of his seed in my greedy channel. My body trembled with all the pleasure that flowed through me as he gave me even more of his cum. It felt like it would be too much and I would overflow, but his big knot kept it all inside of me.

"My beautiful, brave Mate," Shane murmured as he brushed away a strand of sweaty hair from my forehead. "You took my knot so good."

My pussy squeezed around it involuntarily with his praise, and he groaned in response.

"It feels amazing," I moaned.

It was hard to put into words how good and right it felt to have him inside of me, but I guess that was part of being Mates.

"I can't wait to do that again, and again for the rest of our lives together," Shane said, before kissing me.

I had no idea that this negotiation meeting would turn into meeting my Mate, but I was so happy we had found each other.

THE END

Bonus story: Moving in with the Naga

It was moving day. I hated moving. Every time it felt like I was leaving a part of my life behind, but this time I was also moving forward with my relationship with Ezra. I tried to keep good spirits throughout the day, but every box that left my apartment made me feel melancholic.

When the last box was in the truck, I looked around my empty apartment. It had been the place I'd lived in the longest, and it was hard to say goodbye. Ezra saw the look on my face when he slithered in and immediately pulled me into a hug.

"You doing okay?" Ezra asked.

I buried my face in his chest, inhaling his perfect scent. Moving in together felt like the natural progression of our relationship, a sign that we were on the right path. I loved him, and I wanted to be with him, but it was hard to pick out my emotions.

"It's just..."

"I understand," Ezra said, pulling me even closer.

And I knew he really did understand and didn't resent me in any way. I'd moved a lot as a kid and never felt like I belonged anywhere. With my job as an auditor, I traveled a lot, but after my recent promotion, I would be able to work more from home and stay in the city for longer periods of time.

"Thank you," I mumbled against his shirt.

When we got to our new place and unloaded everything from the two vans, we were alone. It suddenly felt very real. This was going to be our place, our home, just the two of us.

"Want to see the bedroom? They just delivered the bed," Ezra said with a smile.

"Yeah, sure," I said, following him through our hallway.

I touched the walls as I passed through, already thinking about which color I would paint them. I wanted to make this place feel like us, for it to feel like a permanent home where we would be together.

The bed took up most of our small bedroom, but it was gorgeous. It was a custom-made round Naga bed that was big enough for Ezra to curl around me. My straight bed had been too small on both sides with at least a tail or arm hanging out, and his bed had been a small round circle just big enough for him to curl up on. This bed was perfect for both of us.

"What do you think?" Ezra asked, and I could hear the trepidation in his voice.

I had given him complete freedom on the bed. My only requirement was that it had to be big enough for both of us.

"I love it," I said, turning around and letting myself fall on top of it.

The mattress was firm but bouncy, and I could already imagine us breaking it in, in the best way.

"Want to test it out?" I asked.

Ezra growled, slithering on top of me, and I could feel his cock harden against my belly.

"We really should unpack," he said as he nipped at my neck with his fangs.

A shiver of delight washed over me as I moaned softly.

"Just a quickie," I asked, opening my legs so he could slide in between them.

"I can never be quick with you," Ezra groaned as he ground his cocks against my pussy.

"Just one," I begged as I unbuttoned the top of my pants, feeling my pussy clench and produce wetness to ease the way for my Naga.

"One orgasm or one cock?" Ezra asked as his hand slipped in my pants, groaning as he felt how wet I was.

"One orgasm. I always want both of your cock. Please, Ezra, just stuff me with both of your cocks," I moaned as he circled my clit with his finger.

"I can never deny you anything," he groaned as he pulled his cocks out while I pushed down my pants.

"Yes, please Ezra," I moaned as I opened my legs wide to accommodate his wide form.

My Naga grabbed both of his cocks in his hand and slid them over my weeping pussy. He covered himself in my wetness and positioned the tips at my entrance. Before I could beg for it, he pushed inside of me. I moaned as his amazing cocks stretched me, making it burn in the most delicious way.

Every single time he filled me with both his cocks at the same time, it felt like he was carving out space for himself in my pussy. He owned me, body and soul, and I loved everything about him. Inch after delicious inch filled me.

"Ezra," I moaned as he bottomed out inside of me.

He growled low, making shivers of delight wash over me. Slowly, he pulled his cocks out, making my pussy clench to keep them inside. When only the tips of them were inside of me, he pushed back inside of me. Pleasure flowed through me as he filled me with his amazing cocks, but I needed just a little bit more to be able to come.

Ezra knew my body almost better than I did, so without me even having to ask, his tail slid between my legs, circling my clit. I moaned as pleasure sparked with each swipe of his tail and the thrust of his cocks.

"You feel so good wrapped around my cocks, Avery," Ezra groaned as he fucked me with his cocks.

"Yes, Ezra, so good," I moaned in response as I could feel the pleasure rise inside of me.

"Come for me, my love," he groaned, fucking me harder.

His tail made smaller and smaller circles around my clit until it rubbed over it with a maddening pace. My orgasm was barreling towards me, but I wanted Ezra to join me as well. I squeezed my pussy around his cocks, making him hiss with pleasure.

"So big, so hard, so full," I moaned. "All of you feel so good, Ezra, Ezra, Ezra."

I repeated his name like a prayer, making him wild with need. His movements became sloppy and I could feel his cocks throb inside of me, signaling his impending release. A few thrusts later, he hissed low, filling me with his cum, igniting my own orgasm. Pleasure washed over me as his hot seed spurted inside of me as my pussy clenched around his cocks, milking him of all of it. My whole body trembled as pleasure flowed through me.

As the pleasure died down, Ezra slowly pulled out his cocks and a gush of his cum left my pussy. He growled, pushing it back inside, but still, some of it got on our brand-new sheets. I was happy we splurged on the waterproof ones so we could easily wipe the cum off.

"Let's get to some more unpacking, and tonight we can sleep in this bed for the first time," Ezra said, cupping my cheek with a gentle caress.

I stretched out, feeling better already, and smiled at him. "Love the bed already. I can't wait to spend more time with you in it."

Ezra grinned and gave me a quick, passionate kiss. "We are going to have so much fun in this bed, but first some more unpacking."

We worked side by side to unpack most of the boxes in our new house, and slowly it started to feel like a home to me. It was amazing having Ezra by my side and knowing we would share this space together.

By the time we put away half our stuff, the evening came, and we were both bone tired. We got ready for bed, and before I knew it, I was engulfed in my Naga's arms, surrounded by his tail. It felt amazing being cuddled like this by him, but I somehow couldn't sleep yet.

Ezra noticed my restlessness and pulled me closer in his embrace. With his lips on the back of my head, he murmured: "Can't sleep?"

I shook my head, playing with the tip of his tail that rested between my breasts.

"Can I help?" Ezra asked.

I rubbed my ass against his cocks, feeling them wake up with the movement.

"Maybe," I sighed.

"Do you want my cocks again, Avery?" he asked his breath a warm tickle against my ear.

"Yes, one after the other," I moaned, pulling one leg up so he could slide between them.

"You want me to fuck you with my cock, fill up your pussy with my cum and then fuck you with the other, making you so full it will drip out while you sleep?" Ezra asked as he pushed his cocks between my thighs, rubbing the top one over my pussy.

"Yes, please," I moaned, getting wet from his hissed words.

He grabbed my leg, pulling it higher, opening up my pussy to receive his cock. He slicked the top one in my wetness, making me tremble with anticipation. Before I could beg for it, he slipped inside. Inch after delicious inch filled me as Ezra gently bit my earlobe, making shivers of delight wash over me.

"So wet, and hot for me," he groaned.

It was the complete opposite of our earlier fucking. This was a slow dance of seduction, while before it was a wild ride of lust. I loved both ways with him. Ezra fucked me slowly as if he had all the time in the world. Lazily pulling his cock out to gently push back inside of me. Soft gasps and moans left my lips as the pleasure inside of me grew steadily. His hands moved towards my breasts, cupping them with his amazing hands.

"I want you to come around my cock, squeezing the cum out of me with your tight pussy," Ezra hissed.

His tail slithered down to find my clit. My pussy clenched around his cock as he circled my clit, sparking pleasure deep inside of me. I loved this position. I was completely surrounded by my Naga, his hands on my breasts, his tail in between my legs, and one of his cocks buried deep inside of me. His slow thrusts and continued focus on my clit made the pleasure rise.

I gripped my pillow tight as I arched my back to get him even deeper inside of me. Ezra hissed as he touched spots inside of my pussy that sparked even more pleasure. I clenched around him, wanting him to cum deep inside of me, filling him with his cum. He played with my nipples as his tail circled my clit quicker.

"I'm going to come," I moaned as pleasure flowed through me.

"Yes, come for me, squeeze my cock," he hissed as he fucked me harder.

His cock touched a spot inside of me that ignited my orgasm. With a pleasured cry, I came clenching around his cock, making him cum as well. Ezra groaned in my ear as he filled me with his cum. Pleasure washed over me as my body trembled and my pussy clenched around his cock. I loved the feel of his throbbing cock spurting deep inside of me.

Before the pleasure ebbed, he pulled his softening cock out and thrust his hard one inside of me. I cried out as he filled me up again. His movements flowed smoothly with the combination of his cum and my wetness. He pushed inside of me, fucking me even faster as if his first orgasm had made him wild with need.

"Are you going to come again?" Ezra hissed in my ear, and I moaned in response.

It felt too good, too much, too full. I knew his second load would make me feel even fuller and I couldn't wait. It felt like my first orgasm never ended, it just flowed into the next. Ezra hissed low, fucking me like a madman, and in moments my pussy clenched around him again, igniting his orgasm.

Ezra filled me with even more cum, making it spill from my pussy. When he moved to pull out, I stopped him.

"Stay inside of me while I sleep," I murmured, already feeling fatigued takeover.

Ezra kissed me gently, settling in behind me with his arms wrapped around me.

"I love you," he murmured.

"I love you too," I replied.

THE END

Authors Note

Collection 6 is ready and out in the world, and my favorite Bonus Couple is moving in together. I thought it was fun to give a bit more of a domestic vibe for this one and show how much their relationship has progressed since starting these. It is almost two years of writing them and I love them more and more each time I come back to them.

Anyway, I hope you enjoyed the story! Please leave a rating and/or a review if you did.

About the author

Lilith Leana writes what she loves; Monster, fantasy, and sci-fi erotica.

Born and raised in Belgium, she devours ebooks as if it heals her. In her day job she loves to organize, plan and make schedules for other people, but when the night falls she can let loose with her fantasies which star all kinds of Monsters and Human couplings.

YOU CAN ALSO FIND ME on:

New Author Website: https://lilithleana.wordpress.com

New Newsletter! Sign Up to be kept up to date about my new releases, sales, character art, and giveaways: Sign Up Form[1]

Instagram: https://www.instagram.com/lilithleana

Merch Shop: https://payhip.com/LilithLeana

Or you can email me: lilith.leana666@gmail.com

DEAR READER

If you enjoyed this book, please consider leaving a review. Indie writers depend on reviews to keep writing and publishing.

Thank you so much ❤

Lilith

---

1.   https://dashboard.mailerlite.com/forms/533589/95138330138642151/share

Also by the author

Series & Collections

<u>Creature Loving Volume 1: A Monster Erotica Collection</u>[1]
<u>Creature Loving Volume 2: A Monster Erotica Collection</u>[2]
<u>Creature Loving Volume 3: A Monster Erotica Collection</u>[3]
<u>Creature Loving Volume 4: A Monster Erotica Collection</u>[4]
<u>Creature Loving Volume 5: A Monster Erotica Collection</u>[5]
<u>Creature Loving Holidays 1: A Monster Erotica Collection</u>[6]
<u>Grim Lovers 1: An Erotic Fairytale Collection</u>[7]
<u>Grim Lovers 2: An Erotic Fairytale Collection</u>[8]
<u>Grim Lovers 3: An Erotic Fairytale Collection</u>[9]
<u>My Ghostly Lover</u>[10]
<u>My Orc Mate</u>[11]
<u>Marrying the Monsters</u>[12]

---

1. https://books2read.com/u/47gLkj

2. https://books2read.com/u/47VMwA

3. https://books2read.com/u/bW0pk1

4. https://books2read.com/u/3LxQD1

5. https://books2read.com/u/4AaD90

6. https://books2read.com/u/bp6Yyg

7. https://books2read.com/u/4AA7Zp

8. https://books2read.com/u/mZpjNe

9. https://books2read.com/u/3J5B2J

10. https://books2read.com/u/3J6dxJ

11. https://books2read.com/u/3yd90L

12. https://books2read.com/u/baLBdL

Sneak Peak of my Next Story:
Saved by the Ghost

My hands went to his hair to have something to hold on to as he rocked my world. Moans tumbled from my lips as he licked my clit with that deliciously icy tongue. Pleasure rose inside of me, and I could almost taste my climax.

"Yes, Roy, please, don't stop," I moaned as I writhed over the sheets with his mouth on my pussy.

Roy groaned in reply, making pleasurable tremors course through me. He only intensified his attention, licking me like a man starved for ages. My pleasure became bigger, and bigger with each flick and lick of his tongue, until it burst.

I came with a pleasured cry as he kept tasting me. My body trembled as my pussy clenched around nothing, achingly empty. Roy lapped up my release, slowly making me come down from my high.

"Fuck me, please," I moaned as the last tremors of my climax left my body.

I wanted more; I needed more of him, and I craved his cock deep inside of me. After a final swipe of his tongue over my pussy, he crawled up my body. He didn't sweat, but my juices covered his mouth. With a laugh, I wiped them off before pulling him down for a kiss. He faintly tasted of me, and something else. It was hard to pinpoint, as it seemed to be so elusive that I could barely taste it at all.

He distracted me with his cock that was sliding against my wet pussy. I moaned as he coated his length in my wetness and then slid inside of me. Roy was big, and he stretched my pussy just to my comfort level to take all of him. Moans tumbled from my lips as pleasure flowed through me. Slowly he gave me inch after delicious inch, filling me with all of him.

"Yes, Roy," I moaned.

"Fuck, Hailey," he groaned in reply.

"Don't stop, please," I moaned as he held himself still as he bottomed out inside of me.

"Never," Roy grunted as he pulled back and thrust fully into my pussy.

I moaned as pleasure rose inside of me with his amazing cold cock, stretching my pussy and touching every pleasure point inside of me.

"You feel so good, hot, wet, and pulsing around me," Roy groaned as he started fucking me, hard.

"Yes, Roy, harder," I moaned.

His thrusts increased until my body rocked against the wall, and his body pushed me into my mattress. His cock pummeled in and out of me, making pleasure spark with each thrust. It felt so good, too good, and I never wanted it to end.

"Don't stop, don't stop," I moaned on repeat as his cock filled me again and again.

Saved by the Ghost – Coming Soon – 28 September

www.ingramcontent.com/pod-product-compliance
Lightning Source LLC
Chambersburg PA
CBHW021807150726
47989CB00004B/1813